SOMEWHERE ENCHANTED

J.F.T.

SOMEWHERE ENCHANTED

J. F. T.

ISBN: 978-1-69457-480-0

'Right, I'm off', Grettos whispered in her ear. She rolled, adopting an even more uncomfortable-looking sleeping position. He got up gently. It didn't take much time for him to find his shoes, clothes and gear. He knew his way around the house even during the darkest hours, and the glow from his rucksack, which was close to his bedside, helped light things up a little. Of course, the glow could not be seen in the daylight hours. It was still light when they usually went to bed so the glow would not have been noticed by his partner.

He walked to the kitchen, packed up some cheese and bread, and then put them in his girdle pouch. He then proceeded to pour some wine into his drinking horn, which he wore diagonally across his chest.

The weather this side of the world was pleasantly warm all year round, so no coats were ever needed. He walked out of his house, past the sweetly-scented garden, the full moon lighting the road ahead. He walked past fifteen houses before he reached an unkempt forest pathway blocked by overgrown shrubs. This pathway had not been used for many years. Taking a deep breath, he reached into his rucksack and pulled two long cutlass machetes out. They had blunt, rounded tips, and didn't pierce the hardened leather of the sack.

Grettos cleared a path, effortlessly cutting through the bushes as if he had been born wielding blades. The cutlasses rotated in both hands, slicing away everything in their path as he progressed into the forest.

He continued forward until, finally, he felt the fresh and brisk air of the forest upon his face, the sweet scent causing him to slow his quickly rotating blades to a gradual standstill.

He took a deep breath. 'Now that was unexpected', he said, expecting to be greeted by the far more subtle smells that were normally found in woods. He reached for his drinking horn and sipped.

His recent activity didn't leave him out of breath, and not a strand from his white, woolly hair was out of place. 'How can this forest be cursed?' he wondered aloud. 'Don't go in there', he continued, mockingly echoing the words of the village elders. Laughing sardonically, 'Ha!', he finished.

Suddenly, from somewhere out of the darkness, he heard the cackle of a laughing female voice. He reached for his cutlasses immediately.

'You smell sweet flowers and hear sweet laughter, yet you reach for your weapons?' asked the voice. 'Brave warrior', she teased, laughing.

Tightening his grip on his cutlasses, he took another breath and replied, 'It's not every day a man gets to walk into a cursed forest. Especially one that smells so sweet and speaks to him'.

The voice did not respond, but the words of the village elders seemed to echo again in his mind: *Don't go in there.* He turned quickly, running back down the path he had made, then stopped suddenly.

'You coward', he muttered to himself. 'We need more land'. He recalled a conversation he had with his wife a few days before. '…and these warnings from the elders not to go into the forest are making our village cramped!'

'Don't go in there, it's cursed!' she had said. 'My mother told me that, and so did yours, and theirs before them'.

'So we just stay here, while our village grows beyond capacity?' he had responded angrily. 'The sad thing is that I spoke to the other young people, and none will dare go into the forest. They all repeat the same warnings. Well, I'm sick of hearing it, and one of these days I'll go and find out what's beyond those trees'.

'It'll be the end of us', she had replied. When he said nothing, she begged him. 'Promise me, promise me that you won't!' He hadn't responded, just walked out while she sobbed his name over and over again.

He turned around, a determined look on his face as he reached for his drinking horn again, and sipped some wine before proceeding towards the deep part of the forest. His heart would have been racing if not for the sweet aromas, which grew more intense the deeper in he went, and had a great calming effect on his nerves. He also noticed that the deeper he went, the hotter it became; and as he went, he used the rising temperatures to be sure he was on the right track.

The trees were tall, with plenty of leaves; but despite this, the moonlight lit his path. He stumbled here and there, a few missteps over small rocks and branches, but he still held ground. He stopped regularly as he moved along the path to reach into his sack for a shy ribbon and tie it around a tree trunk. Shy ribbons glowed in the dark and were made by the villagers many years ago. They were used to help retrace one's steps when they went deep into the forest at night. Their glow was so strong they could be seen from more than thirty yards away, so he tied one to a tree after the light from the last began to fade.

It had been hours since he entered the forest. *It should have been daylight by now*, he thought, but it was still as dark, and the moon still as full as when he had first entered the woods. He marvelled at this, but shrugged his doubts aside and proceeded, determined to know where this heat, aroma, and voice came from. Then he heard it: a rustling sound, as if something was moving through the bushes. He took out one cutlass. The sound came again, closer this time. He spun, trying to judge which direction it came from. As his back was turned, something crashed into him, knocking him to the ground. He sprang to his knees, but saw nothing.

'Ha ha ha ha!' He heard the woman's laughter again, realising as it faded that his cutlass was gone. He glanced around wildly but couldn't find it. Quickly, he reached into his sack for the other one. 'What?!?' he gasped as he found not one cutlass, but two. He yanked both out, spinning them in his hands, the way he had when he first entered the forest.

The rustling sound began again, and he found himself on the ground, this time on his back.

The laughter echoed in the trees. He was on his feet before it faded, hands empty, frustration and confusion mounting when he found both cutlasses in his sack again. He swung the sack onto his back, leaving them in place.

'Who are you?' he screamed. There was no reply, but he got the hint. He would not be using his cutlasses. *For now, at least*, he thought.

He considered returning to the village, but he had come too far. He still had a few shy ribbons left. *I hope that's enough*, he thought to himself. A little worried, more determined, and now even more curious, he continued to follow the heat and sweet scent. He found it strangely comforting that whatever had hit him had chosen not to injure him or cut his head off with the cutlass. At the very least, it could have kept the tools; but it left him unharmed, only disarmed him and returned the tools to him without injury. It could be mocking him, or it could be a warning. Either way, he chose to take the hint and leave the tools in the bag until he thought it necessary to pull them.

As he walked, he imagined how strong this lady had to be to knock him off his feet. He was more than six feet tall and weighed more than nineteen stones of pure muscle. He had large, strong legs and could carry a sixty-kilogram barrel filled with wine, fruits and meat for two miles up the mountains to feed his parents, grandparents and the rest of his elderly extended family.

The heat was becoming unbearable. He stopped, took off his shirt and put it in his rucksack, then took another sip of wine before proceeding. The deeper he went, the more his mind seemed to slip into a delusional state. The wine, the overbearingly sweet scent, and the intense heat intensified his confusion. His walk now a drunken dance, he drowsily reached for his sack, pulled out a ribbon, and tied it to a tree, coughing as he did so. The scent was too strong, as if someone had locked him in a perfume bottle with the lid tightly sealed. As he finished tying the knot, he slumped to the ground, fading away into sleep.

'Ha ha ha ha!' He could hear her laughter echoing through the trees, the last 'Ha!' as usual, ending on a higher note.

'You shouldn't be here. You should have listened. And now—'. The voice was cut off by a rustling sound; then a clap of thunder echoed through the trees. He jerked awake, heart pounding, a burst of warm showers falling hard from the sky. It was still dark, the moon still full.

As he got up he heard the rustling sound, only this time he could see where it was coming from—a bush right ahead of him. He rose and touched the tree, the ribbon still tightly fastened on, then took off running towards the rustling bushes. These bushes were thicker, so he apprehensively removed his cutlasses from his sack. He cut through the bushes quickly, noticing that the smell became stronger, as did the heat, despite the rain. But he was less drowsy, the sleep seeming to have done him some good. *No more wine, for now at least*, he thought.

Suddenly, a bright light was shining through the bushes, contrasting so heavily with the darkness of the forest that it startled him, and he dropped his tools. As his eyes adjusted, all he could make out were flowers of every sort around him as far as he could see, in colours he had never seen before. The sun—there was no mistaking it, it was suddenly broad daylight—was bright and very hot, and he realised he was sweating. As he bent to pick up his tools, he glanced behind, his neatly- cut path seemed to disappear into darkness. He retraced his steps to check. One step he was in the dark forest, the next in a sunny garden.

The rain had suddenly stopped and the leaves of the dark forest were dry, as if it had never rained at all. He returned to the garden. He didn't know how much of the sweet scents he could take, but he pushed forward. The scent wasn't getting stronger, and the heat, too, remained steady. The longer he stood in the garden, the more accustomed to the scent and heat he became. He was still taking in the view when the thick flowers in front of him began to rustle, as if something was moving beneath them. He followed.

Each time he stopped, flowers would rustle again, and he followed along.

This continued until he came to the foot of a waterfall. He looked back to make sure he hadn't lost his way. The field of flowers was only waist-high, so it was easy to see the dark entrance to the forest from afar.

The laughter sounded again. He looked backed at the waterfall and saw a figure stepping into it. As he approached, he could see it was a lady. Her hair was white like his, but silky and long. She motioned him to join her, then disappeared into the waterfall. He followed. As he passed through the waterfall, he entered a cave whose exit was guarded by a shimmering object that seemed to be a two-ended sword. It rotated with enormous speed in mid-air, held by nothing. It was the only way she would have gone, but there was no way he was going to follow past the sword.

'Who are you?' he shouted.

'Walk through the blade, and if your heart and intentions are pure you will arrive safely on the other side', the voice replied.

He looked for something he could use to test the spinning blade. A long, thick root protruded from outside the waterfall into the cave's entrance, so he cut it using his cutlass. He picked it up, walked towards the blade, and thrust it past the spinning sword. He didn't feel even a slight jolt. Smiling, he pulled the root back expecting to find it intact, but a clean cut marked where the sword had sliced through it.

'I'm to believe that tree had bad intentions?' he screamed.

'The tree has no heart or intentions. It follows a pre-set rule: to grow, and that's it. You are not a tree. You have a mind and heart, and thus intentions. Your forefathers got to this point, saw the blade, and ran back in fear. The few fools who tried to walk past were chopped in half. They saw that, too, and thus the villagers were forbidden to go into the forest', she concluded.

'How many men have tried to cross the blade?' he asked. 'More than my years would have me remember', she replied.

'You can't be that old', said Grettos. A familiar laughter pealed through the cave in response.

'In any case, this place is cursed and I'm returning to my village', he said. 'We'll just have to control our population'.

He stepped back through the waterfall, but it led back to the same cave.

'What is this?' he screamed. He tried again and again, the same thing happening each time. His heart beating fast, he ran through the waterfall, again with the same result. He fell to his knees screaming, 'What does this mean?' The laughter only rang cruelly on in response.

Exhausted and hungry, he sank to the floor of the cave. He ate slowly, then took several large draughts of wine. The wine made in the village was very strong; consuming a full cup in one sitting would poison the blood, and Grettos drank enough to intoxicate himself. Drunk and disoriented, he rose.

'I have to get out of here'. With his first step, he tripped over the root he had thrown on the floor and staggered through the rotating blade.

'Well, would you look at that?!' he gasped, lying on the floor, propping himself up with his forearms. 'Not a scratch!'

He looked around; the land was good, the weather as it was back in Elnubrium.

'We could do with land like this', he said, staring at the fair lady sitting on a rock at the foot of the lake. She wore a white lace gown, and had sharp facial features and big green eyes.

'Isn't that why you are here?' she replied. 'To find some land for the Elnubriumites?' He rose and walked gently towards her.

'I would ask you how you know all these things, but after my experiences since entering the forest, I'm guessing you are just as enchanted—perhaps more so', he said, rubbing his chin.

'Walk with me', she replied.

It was a long walk. They passed large numbers of chickens, cows, pigs, sheep and much more, all looking healthy, well kept, and fat.

'We've been walking for miles and all I see is grassland and animals, no people', he said.

'Isn't it just beautiful?' she replied. They kept walking until they came to a great, sprawling stretch of water— it extended beyond the horizon and seemed to go on forever.

'I've never seen so much sand and angry water in my life', he whispered. 'We only have lakes in Elnubrium'.

Elnubrium was a village surrounded by the highest mountains. No one had ever reached the top of the mountains, which were covered by clouds. Some people lived in the foothills of the mountains, but past a certain level it was uninhabitable. The only known habitable land was to the south, where the cursed forest was.

The lady walked towards the water without a care about the incoming tides. She stuck her hand in the water and pulled something out—a bizarre creature, its body formless and clammy, with countless little appendages wiggling about beneath it.

'What is that creature?' he asked.

'It's called an octopus', she replied. 'The male octopus mates with the female and dies; the female octopus then lives long enough to have her babies, then dies afterward. These two die so hundreds of thousands shall live.

'Go now, your village needs you, and you've been missing for quite a while', she urged.

'But what about all this land? My people need land, and here you have not only land, but food and resources to feed us for generations to come'.

'I showed you the land for a reason. Your people can have it if you complete my quests'.

He glared at her. 'And what quest is that?' he asked.

'Everything in its time. Go now, hurry. Your wife needs you'. With that, she turned and walked away.

He ran for the most part, stopping every now and then to sip some wine. *For energy*, he told himself. When he reached the cave, he wondered how many hours had passed since he first arrived. *It's still daylight*, he thought. *I haven't eaten in ages, and I'm not really hungry.* 'She is powerful', he muttered to himself. He didn't like the idea of walking through the blades, but taking a deep breath he walked through, reaching the other side unharmed.

It was very early in the morning when he arrived back in the village. As he approached his garden, he heard a scream.

'He's alive!' a pretty woman, nearly half his size, rushed down the garden pathway and threw herself into his arms, tears streaming down her face. She kissed, then slapped him, and he put her down quickly.

'What's that for? I was only gone a full day at most, and I told you I will be gone for quite a while', he said, holding a hand to his burning cheek.

'A full day? A full day, he says. You went there, didn't you, to the cursed forest? You went there, and four months was as a day', she finished, staring disapprovingly at him.

'F-four months? That can't be. I haven't eaten or drunk water...that woman...'

'What woman?' his wife asked. 'Who were you with while I was here, crying day and night in fear that the forest had taken your life?'

'We only spoke a few words...it seemed a few hours...I didn't even catch her name, but she had powers... there was a spinning sword protecting her...' he trailed off. 'I have much to tell you. I'm starving for now, let's talk over breakfast. You prepare some food. I'll gather some people together—I want everyone to hear this'.

He went to the houses of his friends and family members, inviting them to eat breakfast at his home.

A lengthy discussion followed, ending with all being curious about what the quest could be. They also told him that after a few days of him being gone they searched the land. Upon reaching the shrubs that previously blocked the entrance to the forest, they noticed a path had been cut. No one dared to venture in, but at least they knew where he went.

'We have something urgent to tell you as well', a man announced. 'You won't believe it, but the elders have passed a rule. It is now law that any couple having more than one child should have any additional children killed. It's horrific!' he concluded.

'Then I must return quickly. We can't have dead babies on our consciences', Grettos replied. 'Whatever the quest is, I will do it. Have any babies been killed yet?' he added.

'Not yet', replied Ona, his wife. 'It starts in ten months' time'.

'Good. God knows how long this journey will take. There's not a minute to spare. I will rest and leave this afternoon'.

'So soon?' she asked.

'I'm glad you're so understanding. I'm blessed with a wife that's not only beautiful but kind and patient'.

'I'll miss you', said Ona.

'I'll miss you, too', he replied.

'Find out what she wants, and let us know', said one of the men gathered around the table.

With that, Grettos said goodbye to everyone, he and his wife departing to rest.

'I hope you have some energy for me', she said as they walked up the stairs. He laughed.

Later, Ona woke him up with a kiss. 'It's time', she whispered.

'Already?' he replied, before he kissed her forehead, and rose to put his clothes on.

He packed his gear again, taking with him some wine, cheese and bread. She walked him to the garden where they hugged and kissed once more, then parted.

Walking through the spinning blades, Grettos saw the lady sitting on the rock by the lake again.

'You knew I'd come back, you know what for, so please tell me now, what is the quest?' he asked.

'You must defeat Toguard, the invisible guard'. As she finished the statement, the blade at the door stopped spinning. It had a long grip in the middle, where the two blades joined together at their pommels to make a single one. Its bearer slowly became visible. He separated the swords and came charging towards Grettos.

'I accept!' yelled Grettos, and their blades clashed. Toguard was a large fellow, bigger than Grettos, with broad shoulders, bushy eyebrows, and long curly hair with very dark skin. He had red eyes, a bull nose ring, two earrings in each ear, and was dressed in a black satin garment. Toguard's hits were heavy, but Grettos' strength, and his cutlasses' firm blades, took the hits, especially when he crossed them together.

Grettos slid under Toguard's legs, then swept them out from under him. Toguard fell over backward, head crashing on the floor, swords falling out of hands. Grettos had won.

Standing over him with his blade to his face, Grettos said to the woman, 'I've completed your quest'.

'Quests', she replied. He looked at her, startled. 'Quests, meaning more than one. Two in total, to be exact. That was your first, and this is your last. Remember the octopus? Well, I gave you that example about the circle of life for a reason. You and your wife must give your lives up for the village to survive and thrive'.

'Excuse me?!' Grettos gasped. Toguard rose, picked up his swords, and stood by his mistress's side.

'I won't play fair should you choose to get violent with my mistress', Toguard added.

'I can freeze him right where he stands, ready for you to chop his head off', she said.

'I have no cause to try to harm any of you, which is more than I can say for you', Grettos responded.

'You must bring your wife here and behead her. Toguard will behead you. This is how the ritual must be conducted. This is the circle of life. You and your wife are the parent octopuses, and you must die so that many young shall live. As soon as you are both dead, the powers protecting the forest will stop. The season of permanent spring will spread throughout the forest and garden, down to this land we are in. The spinning sword guard will come with me to a distant land, and all the lands stretching from the forest to the garden to this land shall be given to your people to inhabit. Even the angry waters', she said mockingly, 'shall belong to your people'.

Tears streamed down Grettos' face. He said nothing, just walked away.

He made his way back to his house. He didn't stop to drink, but merely walked in silence, his tears falling. Ona saw him from afar and ran towards him. At the sight of her, he broke down in tears again.

'What's wrong?' she asked.

Gathering himself together, he asked, 'How long has it been?' 'Three months', she replied.

'Then I must hurry. We, should you wish to come, must hurry', he said.

'We?' she asked.

'Let's go inside. I don't want to tell anyone this bit'.

He told her everything and they cuddled and cried together for a long time.

'What do we tell our families? Our friends?' asked Ona.

'We just tell them the curse of the forest will be lifted in six months and they can test it. I'll tell them we have to wait for them there as part of the deal. I'll tell them I defeated her champion and that's all I needed to do. You are so brave. I love you deeply'.

He ate, rested and went to each of their family members and friends, telling them what he and Ona had discussed. He got home late.

'Are you ready?' he asked.

'As ready as I can be', she said, and smiled. 'Let's go and save our village'.

Halfway through the journey to the forest she stopped, looked him sternly in the face, and said, 'Grettos, promise me one thing'.

'What's that, my love?' he asked.

'That when that blade falls on my neck, you take my head off in one sweep', she responded.

'Darling, don't speak of such things', Grettos said, almost in tears. 'I don't want to suffer, Grettos. Promise me'.

'I promise', he muttered.

When they reached the scented gardens, Ona stopped walking,

allowing her tears to fall freely. 'Life is so beautiful', she said. 'I want you to bury me here underneath these pretty flowers, Grettos'.

'It will be my honour', he replied, smiling half-heartedly. 'Come now, we aren't far'.

They continued on to the waterfall, then reached the cave. Upon entering the cave, he noticed that the exit was clear, the rotating blades gone.

'Come, we've been waiting for you two', said the lady. As they entered, Ona was in awe, not only at the beauty of the lady, but the beauty of the land they stepped into. She stared disapprovingly at the seven-foot giant who stood behind the lady, as he had his blade ready in hand. It was as if

Toguard had been waiting for this moment all his life.

'Kneel at the rock and place your head on it', the lady said coldly. 'And how do we know you will keep your word?' Ona enquired.

'You think if I wanted to kill you I couldn't have sent Toguard to behead you both in your sleep? This is the ritual, this is the circle of life. Now kneel, child', the lady said impatiently.

Grettos couldn't take it any longer. He wanted it over and done with. He grabbed Ona by the arm and led her hastily towards the rock, pulling out his cutlass.

'Wait, wait, I'm not ready!' yelled Ona. 'Kiss me'.

Quivering even at the lips, he bent down and kissed Ona for the last time. 'God forgive us', he said and brought the blade down on her neck.

The woman's laughter cut through the air right before the blade touched Ona's neck.

Grettos found himself on the ground, the blade gone from his hand.

Ona was unharmed and Grettos disarmed, yet again. Toguard then reappeared, walking back to his mistress, Grettos' cutlasses in his hand. He had been the one disarming Grettos all along.

'Do I look like a monster to you, boy?' the lady asked.

'Ho ho ho!' Toguard laughed. 'You should have seen your face!' he added in a strange accent. The lady slapped his arm.

'Shut up, Toguard', she said.

'What does this all mean?' Grettos asked, as he joyously helped Ona to her feet.

'It means you pass my final test. You are both pure in heart and would have died for your people. You would make a good king and queen. Long live the King and Queen of the Great Lands. It's all yours, as promised.

'Come, Toguard, we have more fish to fry in distant lands', she added, as the lady and Toguard walked off.

Grettos and Ona stood in disbelief and shock.

'I didn't catch your name!' screamed Grettos, finally managing to say something.

'That's 'cause I didn't throw it, darling'.

'Ho ho ho, throw it, good one', said Toguard. 'Shut up, Toguard'.

The End